JIM SMITH
The Frog Band and the Onion Seller

A WORLD'S WORK CHILDREN'S BOOK

Text and illustrations © 1976 by Jim Smith. All rights reserved.
First published by World's Work Ltd, The Windmill Press, Kingswood, Tadworth, Surrey
Printed in Great Britain by William Clowes & Sons, Limited, London, Beccles and Colchester
SBN 437 75903 2

Once upon a time, there lived in a tumbledown chateau the Duke de Buffo Buffo. He was very aristocratic, and like all aristocratic Dukes who live in tumbledown chateaux, he was very poor. One day, he was up in the attics looking for something of value he could sell. All he was able to find was a piece of parchment and a rusty key, in the bottom of a trunk, under some old books. This wasn't surprising, as he had searched the attics almost every day for years. He was about to throw the parchment away in disgust, when to his amazement, he saw it was a map, showing a large house in England, and directions to a hidden casket containing treasure! The Duke could hardly believe his eyes!

With great excitement, the Duke rushed downstairs, too thrilled to notice the nail on the stair-treads. "Yeow!" he cried, and hobbled painfully to his bedroom. As he sat on his bed, bandaging his foot, he decided on a plan of action. . . .

He was too old to go off across the sea on a treasure hunt, and besides, his foot hurt. So, he realised he would have to enlist the help of that eminent detective – Alphonse le Flic.

Alphonse came immediately, and took down all the details in his pocket-book. As soon as he had said "*Au revoir*" to the Duke, he dived behind a nearby bush and re-appeared disguised as a typical French onion-seller, complete with bicycle and onions.

He crossed the Channel, heading for
Winklesea, with his bicycle strapped
securely to the top of his submarine.
When land was in sight, he made for
the pier, and having tied up his
submarine, he set foot, un-noticed,
on English soil.

He looked at his map, and set off, wondering as he wobbled along on the wrong side of the road why everyone was shouting at him. As he swung round a corner, a lorry-load of frogs swerved to avoid him and landed up in a fruit-barrow. Alphonse pedalled swiftly on, leaving the angry frogs behind.

Unbeknown to Alphonse, the frogs belonged to the Frog Band, who were due to play on the sea-front. As Alphonse pedalled into the distance, they picked themselves up and went on their way, muttering dire threats if they ever saw the French frog again – "I'll clash him between my cymbals – I'll give him such a trumpeting – You wait, I'll cornet him."

Alphonse hummed to himself in tune with the music coming from the sea-front. As he drew level with the bandstand, the music suddenly stopped and Alphonse saw, to his horror, a horde of red-coated frogs coming towards him, shouting and shaking their fists at him.

Alphonse rode for all his worth towards the large house on the hill, spurred on by the threats of the Frog Band. When he reached the gates, he propped his bicycle up against the wall, and entered the court-yard, to find himself in a monastery. The monks took no notice of him, so, after a quick check on the map, he darted towards the kitchen.

Inside, the rather dismal Brother Borzoi was washing a pan. He looked up
just in time to see a striped jumper disappear down his cellar steps.
By this time, the Frog Band, still hot in pursuit of Alphonse, had invaded the
court-yard. They stopped in awe when they saw all the monks. "Where is he?
Where is the onion-seller?" demanded Johann S. Frog, the Band Leader.

Father Abbot, not surprisingly, looked slightly blank, but just then Brother Borzoi came running out of the kitchen. "Do you mean a fellow in a striped jumper?" he asked Johann, "You'll find him in my cellar!" "Follow me, Frogs!" yelled Johann and headed for the cellar steps.

Meanwhile, Alphonse had produced a candle from under his jumper, and was following the old Duke de Buffo Buffo's plan. "Left turn, down steps. Four paces on, turn right, six steps. Now, three stones left from the ring in the wall and PUSH!"

With a hideous grating noise, the stone block swung out of the wall on rusty hinges. Shielding his candle from the sudden gush of air, Alphonse peered into the gloomy depths. He could just make out a stream of water running down the floor of the tunnel. On a ledge above the water level, there was an old iron-bound casket.

"The treasure! I've found it!" gleefully whispered Alphonse, and he jumped through the hole, picked up the casket and was just about to go back through to the cellar when he heard the angry voices and the scrambling feet of the approaching frogs. Losing no time, Alphonse waded along the tunnel. As he struggled through the water, he saw rusty handholes in the wall, leading up to a bright circle of daylight.

Dropping his candle, he clambered up,
to find himself on the top of the cliff,
outside the monastery wall.
Below him, Johann S. Frog and Brother
Borzoi were looking into the secret
opening. Silently they watched
Alphonse's candle float by. "Bless his soul,"
murmured the monk, with bowed head.
"I think we need look no further."

By now, Alphonse had made his way back to the gates and found his bicycle. He tied the casket to the carrier, and, with a backward glance, pedalled furiously towards the pier and France.

While Alphonse and the rest of the Frog Band had been playing hide-and-seek in the monastery, Shortie Frog was still labouring up the hill. "I wish the others would wait for me just once," he puffed as he clutched his tuba to him. Alphonse, on seeing yet another frog coming towards him, muttered "Oh no! Where do all these frogs come from?" and quickly headed off the road down a turning.

But it was too late! Shortie had seen him and immediately found his voice. "I say you fellows! Over here! I've found him!" At the sound of the rallying blast on his tuba, the Frog Band poured out of the monastery gates, passing Shortie. "Wait for me," cried Shortie, "Hey, wait!" Down the road went Alphonse, pedalling frantically, and down the road followed the Frog Band.

At last Alphonse sighted the pier. "What luck," he panted as he shot on down the hill. At the entrance to the pier, he braked hard as two rats came across the road, carrying their up-turned boat between them. "HELP!" cried Alphonse, "What a time to find my brakes don't work. Get out of the WAY!"

But the rats were too slow, and they watched open-mouthed as Alphonse and his bicycle hit the boat, shot up the sloping hull, and landed upright on the other side of the pier entrance. "Phew!" breathed Alphonse as he sped on to the end of the pier and shot over the edge, sending up a sheet of water.

Johann S. Frog and the Frog Band arrived breathless at the pier, and joined
the crowds looking on unbelievingly as a string of onions slowly floated to the
surface. "Throw a lifebelt someone! We may yet be able to save him!"
ordered Johann. Unconcerned, Alphonse swam strongly underwater towards
his submarine, clutching his bicycle and the precious casket.

With his bicycle once again lashed to the top, he started the submarine's motor and surfaced. "*Au revoir* my friends," he cried to the dumb-founded frogs, "*Au revoir!*" and with a wave of his beret, he steered his submarine towards the French coast. The Frog Band hauled in the lifebelt, still not sure how Alphonse had escaped, but glad he was alive.

WHAT
THE
STOAT
SAW
1D

Back in the chateau, Alphonse wheeled his bicycle up the stairs to the Duke de Buffo Buffo's bedroom. The Duke hobbled forward excitedly and grasped the casket from the detective. With eager, shaking hands, he fitted the key into the lock.

The poor Duke was horror-stricken as the lid flew open to reveal, not priceless treasure, but worthless rubbish! Furious, the Duke rushed towards Alphonse, roaring "You silly frog!" and kicked him out of the window.

"OOOOh!" he yelled as he hit the bicycle with his bad foot, and he threw it after Alphonse out of the window.

The unfortunate detective came round to find himself on the lawn with his bicycle, and was just recovering when CRASH! the casket landed beside him. The bemused Alphonse suddenly shouted with glee as the casket cracked, the sides split, and on to the grass rolled twenty large gold coins!

"We're rich, Alphonse!" yelled down the Duke from the window. "It's like a story! We can live happily ever after!"

 S0-DTD-720

RICHARD SCARRY'S

BUSY KIDS
Learn to Count!

Featuring new illustrations
by Huck Scarry

RiverStream

RiverStream Publishing and the distinctive RiverStream Publishing logo
are registered trademarks of RiverStream Publishing, Inc.

Copyright © 2013 Richard Scarry Corporation, all illustrations.
Copyright © 2013 Dancing Penguins, LLC/JR Sansevere, all text.

All characters are property of Richard Scarry Corporation.

All rights reserved. No part of this publication may be reproduced, stored in a retrieval system, or
transmitted, in any form or by any means, electronic, mechanical, photocopying, recording, or
otherwise, without prior written permission from the publisher. Purchase of this book for
classroom use allows pages to be reproduced for classroom use only.

ISBN 978-1-62243-088-8

Published in 2013 by RiverStream Publishing Company, Inc.
By arrangement with Dancing Penguins, LLC
On behalf of the Richard Scarry Corporation

Library of Congress Cataloging-in-Publication Data on file with the Publisher.

 a Dancing Penguins • J R Sansevere Book

Written by Erica Farber
Edited by Tracey Dils
Designed by Matthew Rossetti
Covers designed by Gina Fujita

1 2 3 4 5 GPP 15 14 13 12

RiverStream Publishing—Globus Printing & Packaging
Minster, OH—122012—1001GPPF12

www.riverstreampublishing.net

Meet the Busy Kids of Busytown!

Froggy

Lowly

Bridget

Huckle

Arthur

Ella

Molly

Frances

Skip

Miss Honey

My Name _____

Which is Biggest?

Beep! Beep! The cars and trucks race! Color the biggest object in each row red.

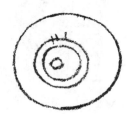
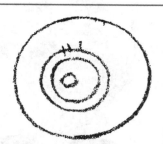

My Name

Which is Smallest?

Zoom! Zoom! Color the smallest object in each row green.

My Name

Small, Medium, and Large

Vroom! Vroom! Don't forget to check your brakes. Color the biggest object in each row blue. Color the smallest object in each row red. Color the medium object in each row yellow.

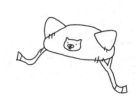
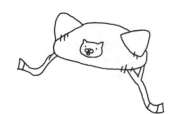
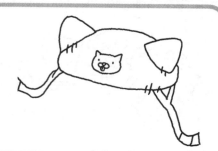

Heavier and Lighter

Cars and trucks come in all shapes and sizes. Color the heavier object red. Color the lighter object blue.

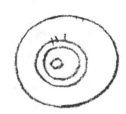

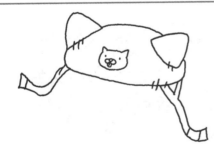

Longer and Shorter

Some cars are long, some cars are short. Color the longer car yellow. Color the shorter car green.

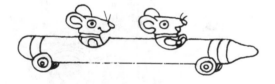

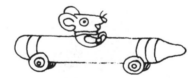

Shapes

The race is on! Color the triangles yellow. Color the circles green. Color the squares blue.

Shape Search

Zoom! Zoom! Keep your eye on the road! Circle the triangles. Put a check mark on the circles. Put an X on the squares.

What's the Same?

Take good care of your cars and trucks. Circle the objects in each column that are the same as the object at the top of the column. The first one has been done for you.

Sorting

Squeak! Squeak! Time for a tune-up. Draw a line from each object that belongs in the toolbox to the toolbox.
Scrub-a-dub-dub! Draw a line from each object that belongs in the cleaning bucket to the bucket.

Sorting

Beep! Beep! Drive carefully! Circle the 8 objects that don't belong at the racetrack.

Count 1, 2, 3!

One, two, three, go! Count out loud the number of cars in each square. Then color the correct number.

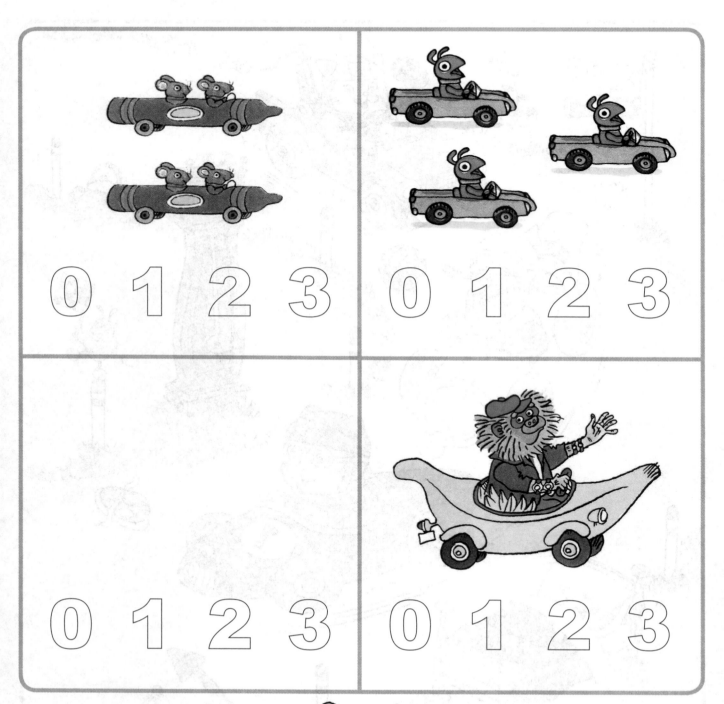

0 1 2 3   0 1 2 3

0 1 2 3   0 1 2 3

Count 1, 2, 3!

Silly Arthur, you can only wear one helmet at a time! Count the objects in each row. Then draw a line from the objects to the correct number.

2

3

1

Writing 0, 1, 2, 3

Only two mice fit in a two-seater crayon car. Please wait for the next car. Trace the numbers below. Then write them on the blank lines.

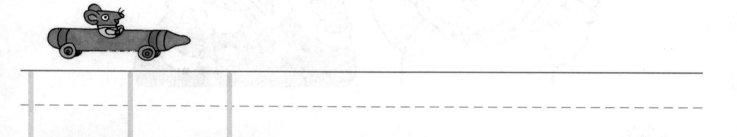

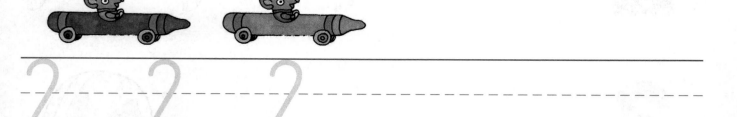

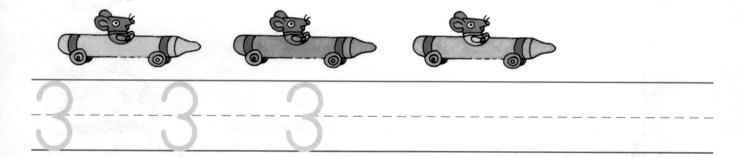

First, Second, and Third

Draw a circle around the car that matches the word—first, second, third!

first

third

second

first

First, Second, and Third

Come on, Arthur! It's time to race! Color the car that is first, blue. Color the car that is second, red. Color the car that is third, yellow.

FINISH

Counting 4, 5

Look out for the safety cones! Count the number of objects in each group. Then color the correct number.

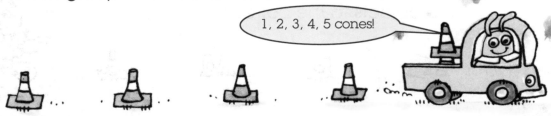

1, 2, 3, 4, 5 cones!

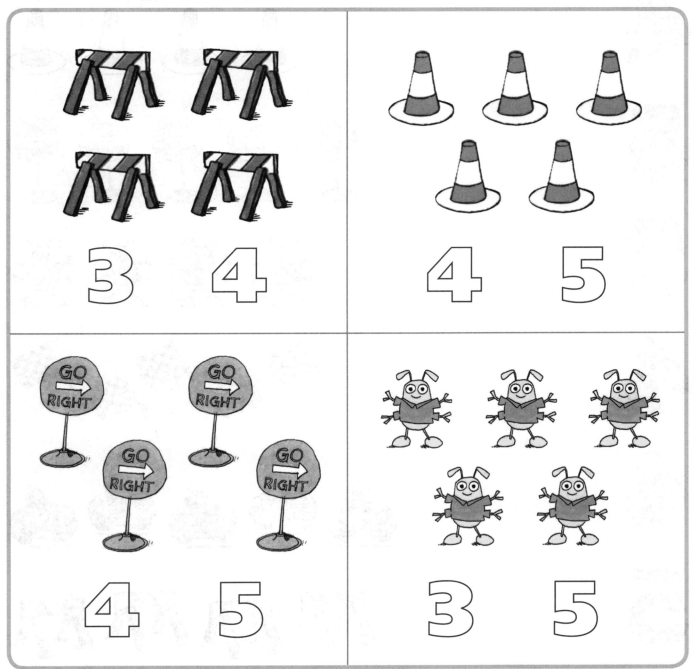

Counting 4, 5

Goldbug is very busy at the race! Count the objects in each row. Then draw a line from the objects to the correct number.

4

5

5

4

4

5

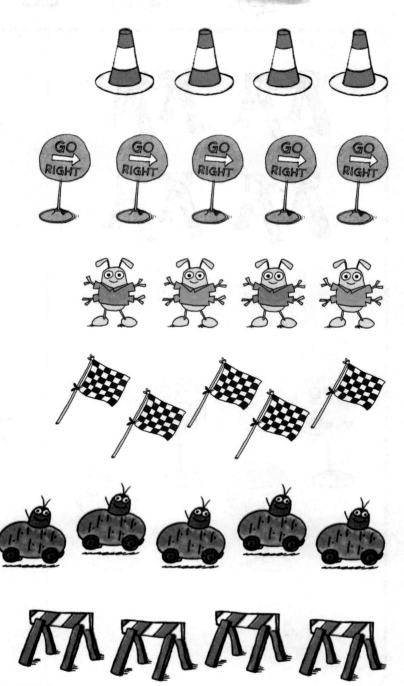

Writing 4, 5

Watch those wheels, Molly! Trace the numbers below.
Then write them on the lines.

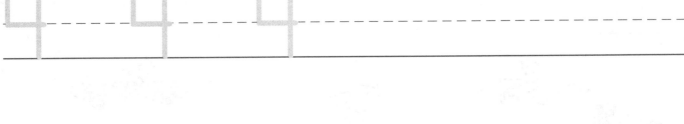

4 4 4

5 5 5

Counting 1-5

Pencil cars are fun to ride in! Count the number of cars in each square. Then color the correct number.

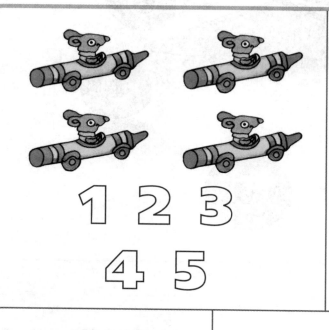

1 2 3
4 5

1 2 3
4 5

1 2 3
4 5

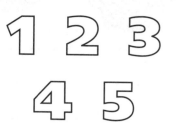

1 2 3
4 5

1 2 3
4 5

Counting 1-5

Count the objects in each square. Write the correct number on the line under each picture.

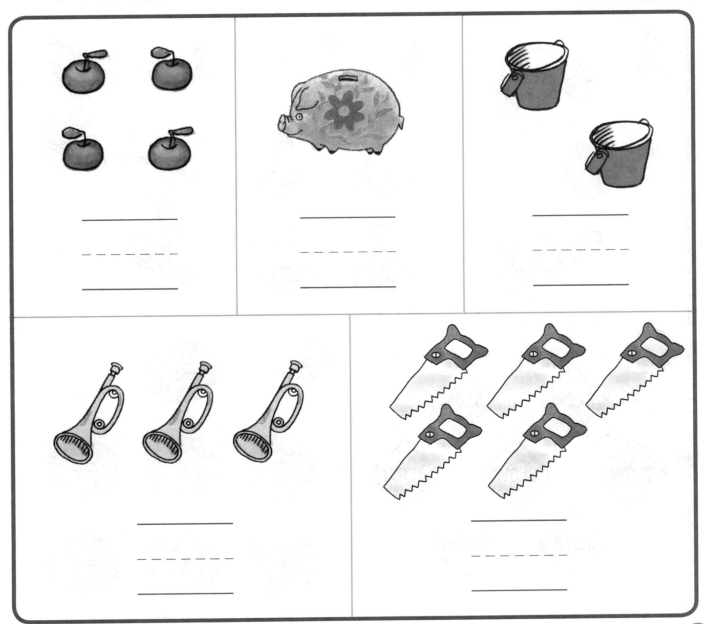

Counting 1-5

Go, Huckle, go! Draw a circle around the number of objects in each group to match the correct number. The first one has been done for you.

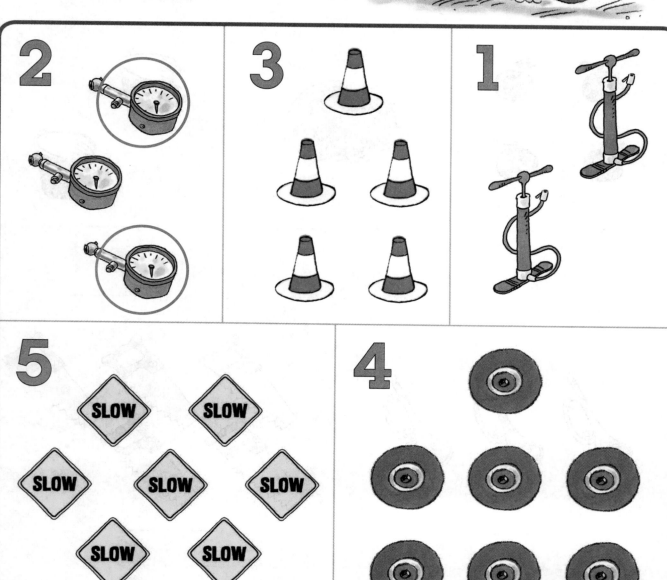

Counting 6, 7

Crash! Skip was going too fast! Count the number of objects in each square. Then color the same number.

5   6

6   7

6   7

5   7

Counting 6, 7

See Goldbug cheer on the racers. Go, racers, go! Count the objects. Then draw a line from the objects to the correct number.

Go! Go! Go!

6

7

7

6

6

7

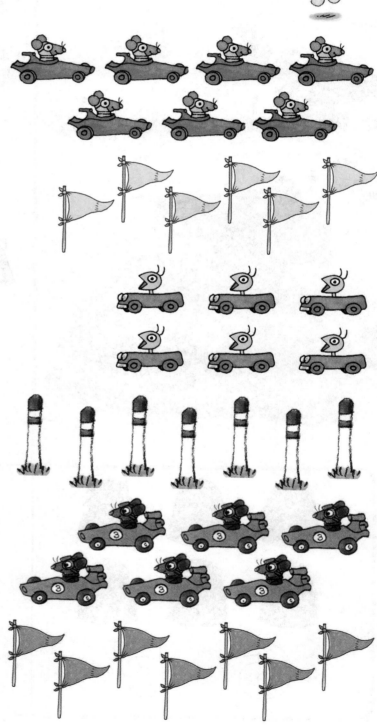

Writing 6, 7

Candy makes Frances go fast! Trace the numbers below.
Then write them on the lines.

6 6 6

7 7 7

Counting 8, 9

Don't worry, Ella! Huckle and Lowly will pull you out of the mud!
Count the number of objects in each box. Then color the
same number.

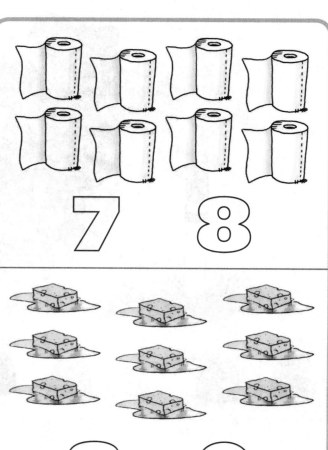

7   8

8   9

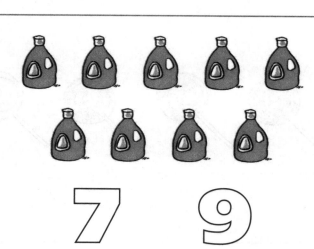

8   9

7   9

Counting 8, 9

Huckle and his friends like to ride the bus to school. Count the objects. Then draw a line from the objects to the correct number.

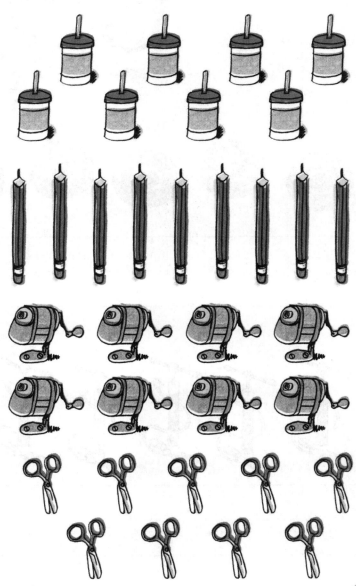

Writing 8, 9

Huckle pumps air into his tire. Stop, Huckle, stop! Your tire will pop! Trace the numbers below. Then write them on the lines.

8   8   8

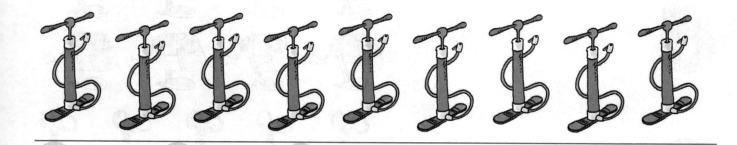

9   9   9

Counting to 10

Lowly helps Huckle put out safety cones. Careful, Lowly!
Count the number of cones in each box. Then color the
same number.

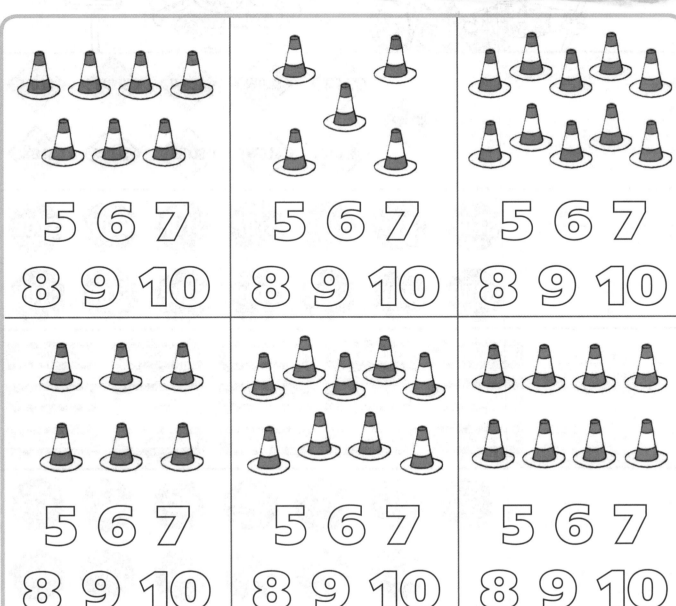

Writing 10

Bridget thinks Goldbug is going too fast. Watch out, Goldbug! Trace the number 10. Then write 10 on the lines provided. Next, cross out the objects in each group so there are ten things left.

What Comes Before?

Help Huckle and Lowly find the correct speed limits. In the blank space in each box, write the number that comes before the number shown. The first one has been done for you.

SPEED LIMIT
2 3

SPEED LIMIT
___ 4

SPEED LIMIT
___ 5

SPEED LIMIT
___ 6

SPEED LIMIT
___ 7

SPEED LIMIT
___ 8

SPEED LIMIT
___ 9

SPEED LIMIT
___ 10

33

What Comes After?

More speed limit signs are missing! Help Goldbug find them. In the blank space in each box, write the number that comes after the number shown. The first one has been done for you.

SPEED LIMIT **1** 2	SPEED LIMIT **2**

SPEED LIMIT **3**	SPEED LIMIT **4**	SPEED LIMIT **5**
SPEED LIMIT **6**	SPEED LIMIT **7**	SPEED LIMIT **8**

Counting 1-10

Huckle, Lowly, and Bridget like to count forward and backward! Help them fill in the missing numbers.

Listen to us count backward!

1, 2, 3, 4, 5...

...6, 7, 8, 9, 10!

1 ☐ 3 ☐ 5 6 7 ☐ 9 10

1 2 ☐ 4 ☐ 6 7 8 ☐ 10

1 ☐ 3 4 5 ☐ 7 8 ☐ 10

☐ 2 3 4 5 6 ☐ 8 9 ☐

Get it?

We were facing backward when we were counting!

Counting Backward

Hee! Hee! Lowly likes to tell number jokes. Miss Honey wants him to write his numbers, too. Help Lowly fill in the missing numbers.

10 9 ☐ 7 6 5 4 3 2 1

10 9 8 ☐ 6 5 4 ☐ 2 1

10 9 ☐ 7 6 5 4 3 ☐ 1

10 ☐ 8 7 ☐ 5 ☐ 3 2 1

Which Number Is Greater?

Lowly has another number joke. "Ha! Ha! Ha!" laughs Huckle. Which group has more objects? Circle the number that is greater. The first one has been done for you.

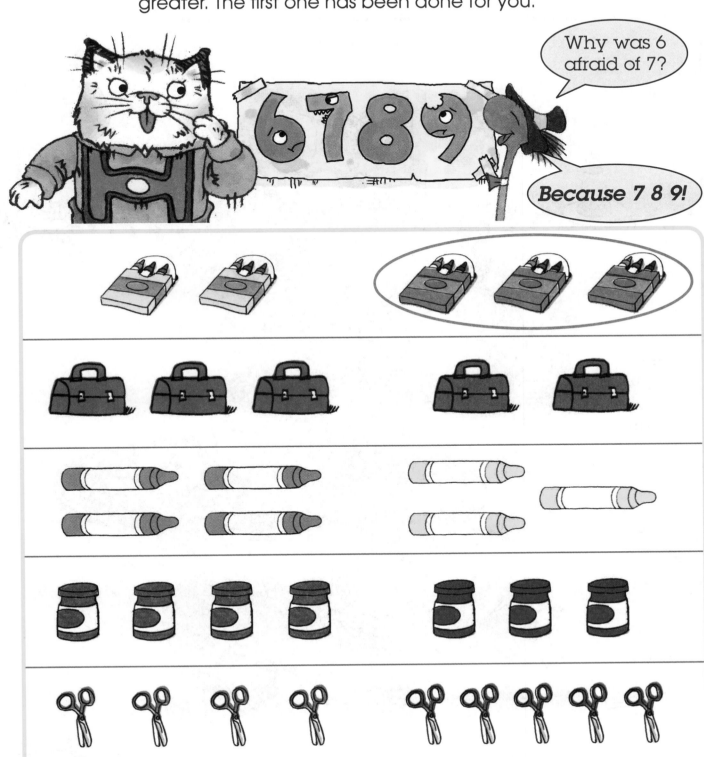

How Many?

See the racers go! Count how many flags, cars, safety cones and racers are on both pages. Then circle the correct number.

flags	1	2	3	cars	7	8	9
cones	4	5	6	racers	8	9	10

Which Group Has Fewer?

Oh, no! Arthur's stuff is falling out of his car! Now he has less in his car than out of it. In each row below, circle the group that has fewer objects. The first one has been done for you.

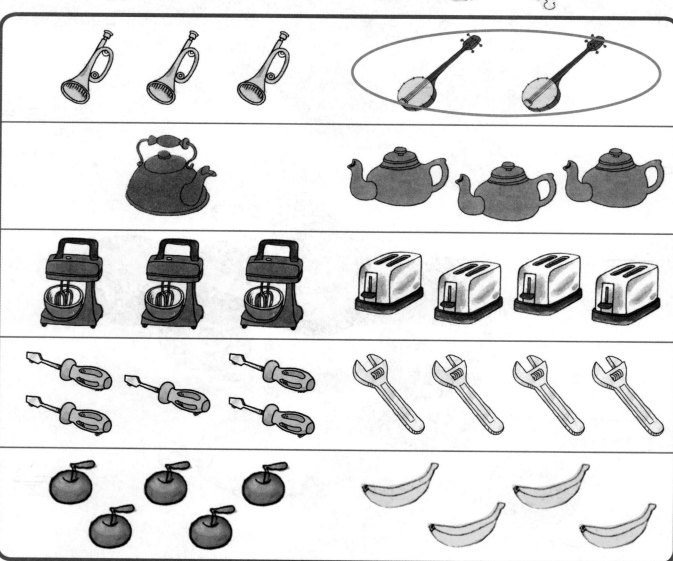

Which Group Has Fewer?

It's not safe to read and drive, Molly! Look out! Circle the group that has fewer objects. The first one has been done for you.

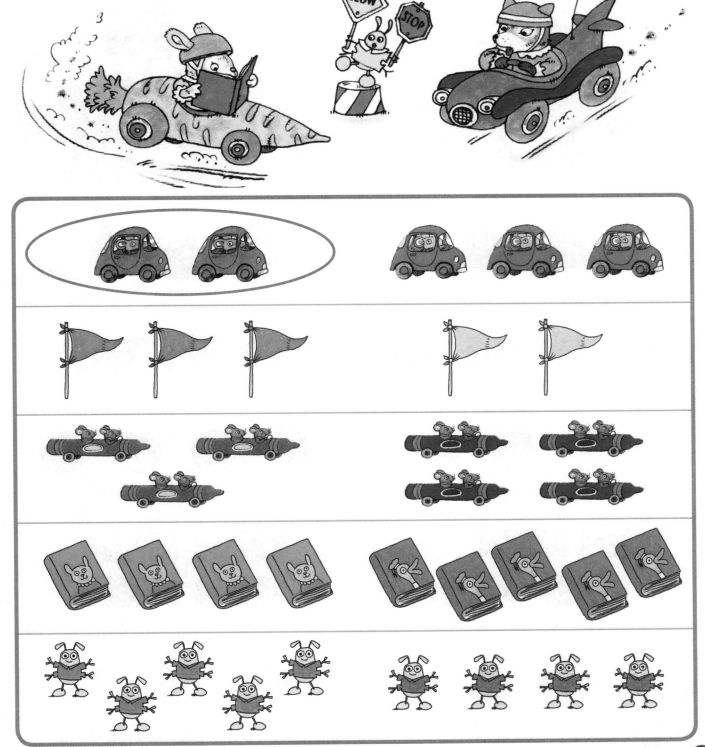

Which Group Has More?

Oh, no! Frances's car is losing a little candy. Now it's losing a lot of candy! In each of the rows below, circle the group that has more candy. The first one has been done for you.

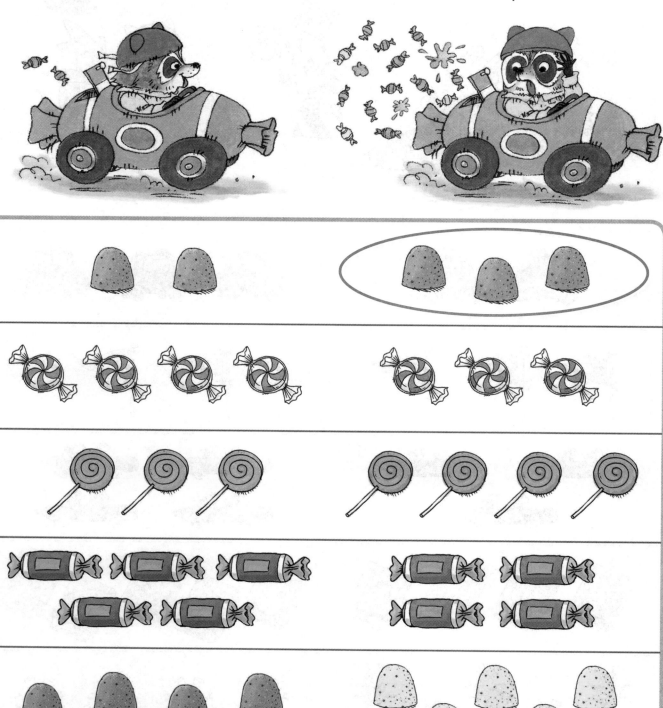

What Comes Next?

Look out! Lowly is making patterns with shapes and he just broke the chalk! In the row below, color the shape that comes next in the pattern. The first one has been done for you.

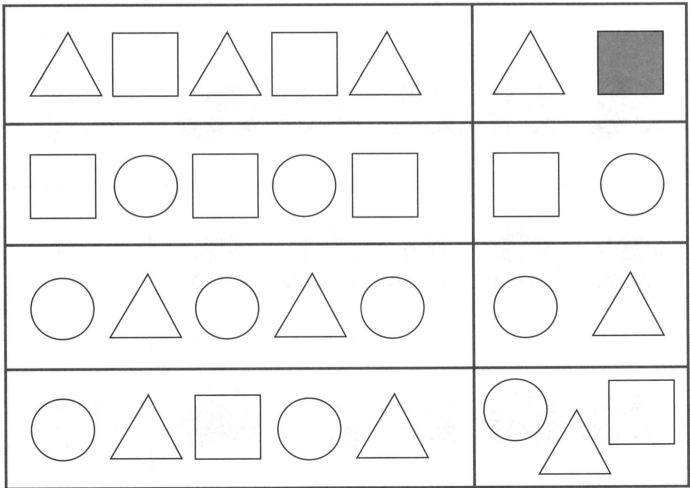

My Name

What Comes Next?

Ella is behind Bridget, and Molly is behind Ella. Who is next? Goldbug! Color the car that comes next in the patterns below. The first one has been done for you.

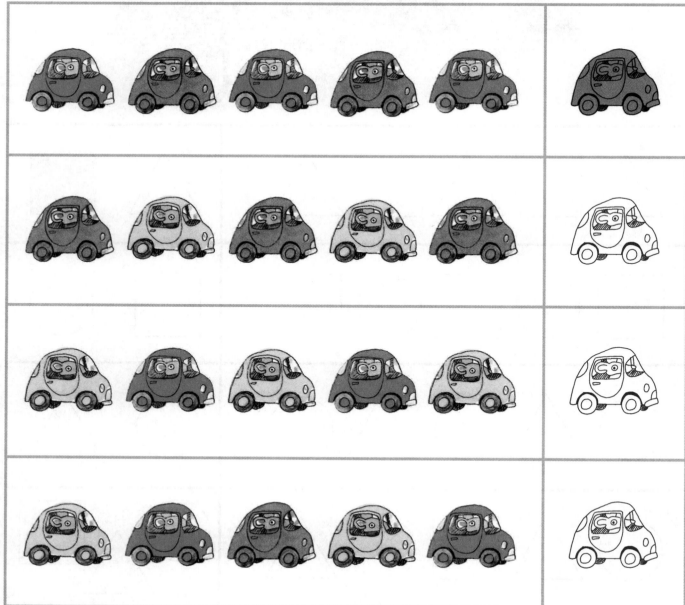

44

Above, Below, and Next to

Today is race day—hooray! Circle the objects that are above Huckle. Put an X on the objects that are next to Huckle. Put a check mark on the objects that are below Huckle. Use the checklist to help you.

Object Checklist:	chair	clock	airplane
	poster	box	bed
	ball	backpack	train

Above, Below, and Next to

Yippee! Huckle and Lowly win the race! Circle the objects that are above Lowly. Put an X on the objects that are next to Lowly. Put a check mark on the objects that are below Lowly. Use the checklist to help you.

Object Checklist:	pole	flower	safety cone
	banner	bird	Goldbug's flag
	leaf	butterfly	post

Graphing

Help! The race is about to start! Does Goldbug have everything ready? Count the objects in each group. Then color the same number of squares in that row. The first one has been done for you.

(4 cones)	░	░	░	░	
(cat flag)					
(5 batons)					
(2 trophies)					
(3 flags)					

Graphing

Time to race! First, Huckle makes sure he has all of his tools.
Count the objects in each group. Then color the same number
of squares in that column. The first one is done for you.

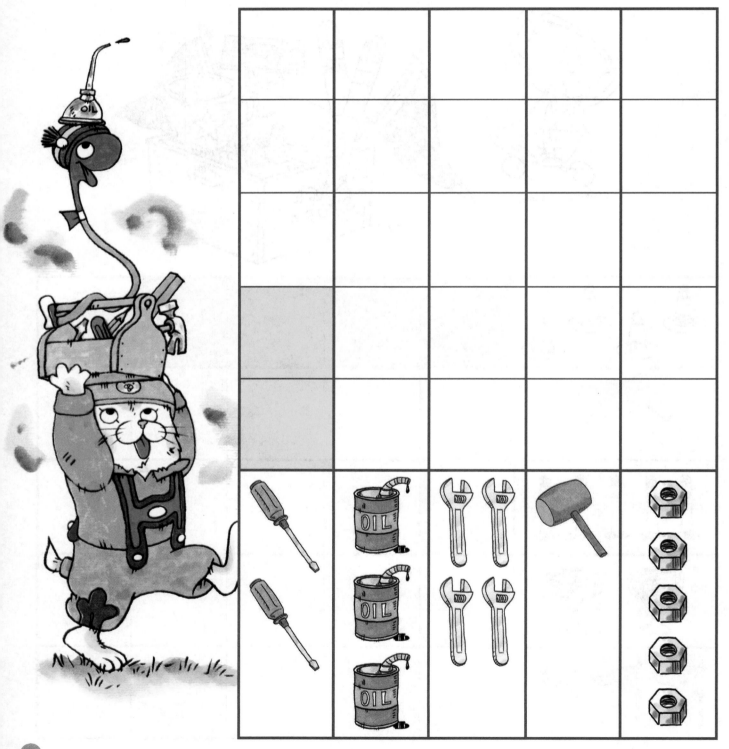

My Name

Addition with Sums Up to 4

Count how many objects are in the first group. Write the number under the picture. Count the objects in the second group. Write the number under the picture. Now count the objects in both groups together. Write the number in the box. The first one has been done for you.

1 + 1 = 2

___ + ___ =

___ + ___ =

___ + ___ =

My Name _____

Addition with Sums Up to 5

Count how many objects are in the first group. Write the number under the picture. Count the objects in the second group. Write the number under the picture. Now count the objects in both groups together. Write the number in the box. The first one has been done for you.

1 + 2 = 3

___ + ___ = ☐

___ + ___ = ☐

___ + ___ = ☐

Subtraction Through 4

Molly likes to play jacks! She picks some up and some are left.
Count the total number of objects. Then count the number of
objects that are not crossed out. That is the number of objects
left. Write the number in the box. The first one has been done
for you.

4 - 2 = 2

___ - ___ =

___ - ___ =

___ - ___ =

Subtraction Through 5

Bye-bye! The cars are driving away! Count the number of cars that are not crossed out. That is the number of cars that are left. Write the number in the box. The first one has been done for you.

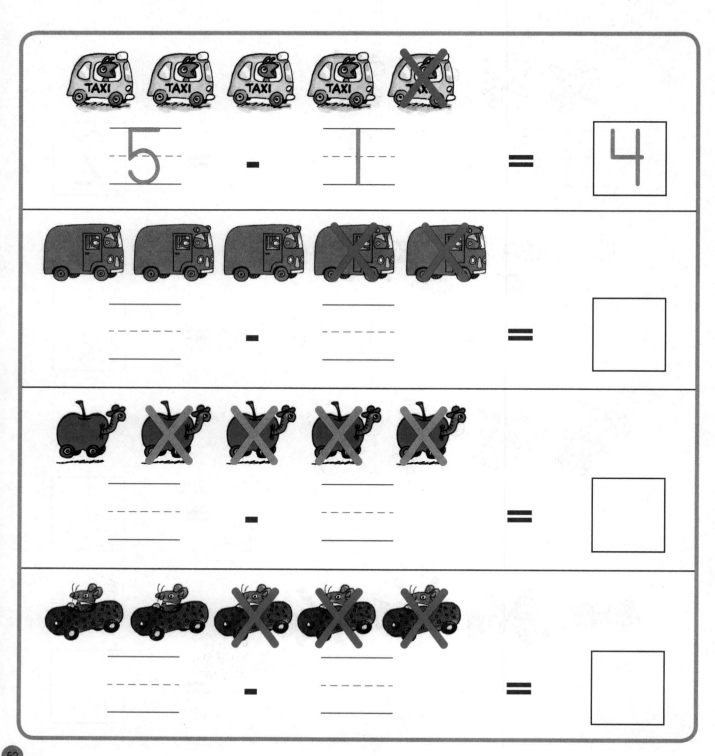

5 - 1 = 4

___ - ___ = ☐

___ - ___ = ☐

___ - ___ = ☐

Which is Biggest?

Beep! Beep! The cars and trucks race! Color the biggest object in each row red.

Which is Smallest?

Zoom! Zoom! Color the smallest object in each row green.

Small, Medium, and Large

Vroom! Vroom! Don't forget to check your brakes. Color the biggest object in each row blue. Color the smallest object in each row red. Color the medium object in each row yellow.

Heavier and Lighter

Cars and trucks come in all shapes and sizes. Color the heavier object red. Color the lighter object blue.

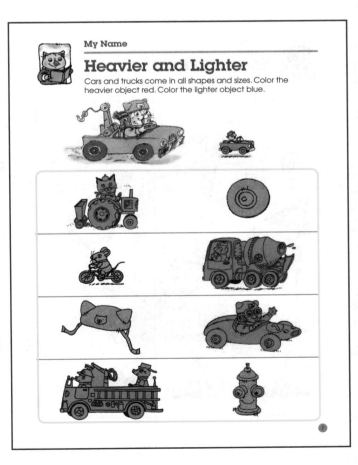

Longer and Shorter

My Name _____

Some cars are long, some cars are short. Color the longer car yellow. Color the shorter car green.

Shapes

My Name _____

The race is on! Color the triangles yellow. Color the circles green. Color the squares blue.

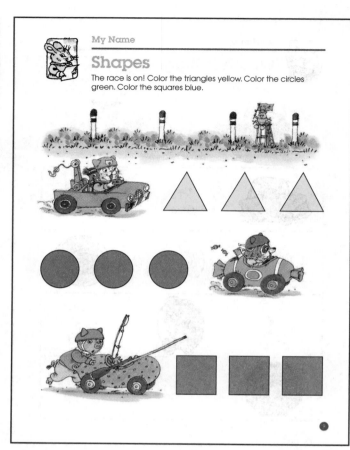

Shape Search

My Name _____

Zoom! Zoom! Keep your eye on the road! Circle the triangles. Put a check mark on the circles. Put an X on the squares.

What's the Same?

My Name _____

Take good care of your cars and trucks. Circle the objects in each column that are the same as the object at the top of the column. The first one has been done for you.

Sorting

Squeak! Squeak! Time for a tune-up. Draw a line from each object that belongs in the toolbox to the toolbox.
Scrub-a-dub-dub! Draw a line from each object that belongs in the cleaning bucket to the bucket.

Sorting

Beep! Beep! Drive carefully! Circle the 8 objects that don't belong at the racetrack.

Count 1, 2, 3!

One, two, three, go! Count out loud the number of cars in each square. Then color the correct number.

Count 1, 2, 3!

Silly Arthur, you can only wear one helmet at a time! Count the objects in each row. Then draw a line from the objects to the correct number.

Writing 0, 1, 2, 3

Only two mice fit in a two-seater crayon car. Please wait for the next car. Trace the numbers below. Then write them on the blank lines.

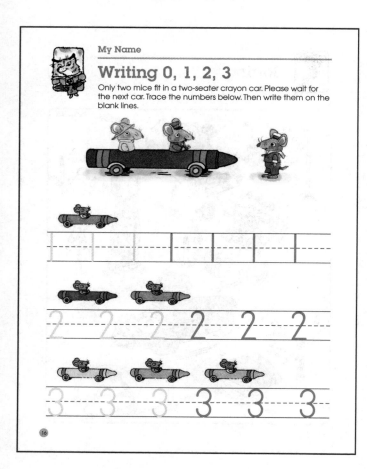

First, Second, and Third

Draw a circle around the car that matches the word—first, second, third!

First, Second, and Third

Come on, Arthur! It's time to race! Color the car that is first, blue. Color the car that is second, red. Color the car that is third, yellow.

Counting 4, 5

Look out for the safety cones! Count the number of objects in each group. Then color the correct number.

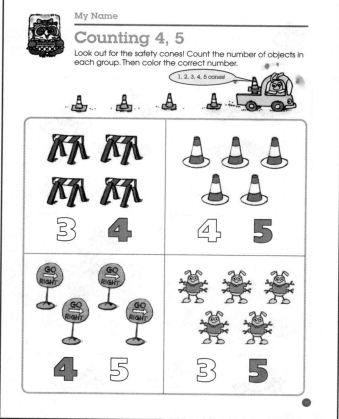

My Name

Counting 4, 5

Goldbug is very busy at the race! Count the objects in each row. Then draw a line from the objects to the correct number.

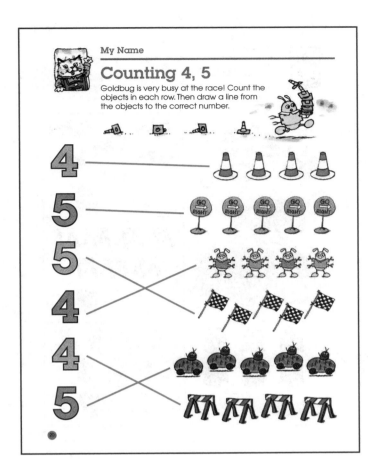

My Name

Writing 4, 5

Watch those wheels, Molly! Trace the numbers below. Then write them on the lines.

My Name

Counting 1-5

Pencil cars are fun to ride in! Count the number of cars in each square. Then color the correct number.

My Name

Counting 1-5

Count the objects in each square. Write the correct number on the line under each picture.

My Name _____

Counting 1-5

Go, Huckle, go! Draw a circle around the number of objects in each group to match the correct number. The first one has been done for you.

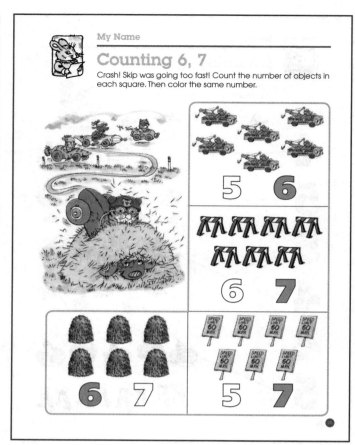

My Name _____

Counting 6, 7

Crash! Skip was going too fast! Count the number of objects in each square. Then color the same number.

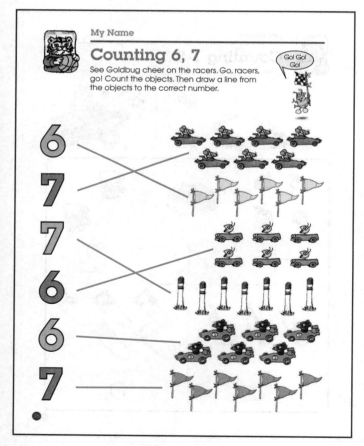

My Name _____

Counting 6, 7

See Goldbug cheer on the racers. Go, racers, go! Count the objects. Then draw a line from the objects to the correct number.

Go! Go! Go!

My Name _____

Writing 6, 7

Candy makes Frances go fast! Trace the numbers below. Then write them on the lines.

My Name _____

Counting 8, 9

Don't worry, Ella! Huckle and Lowly will pull you out of the mud! Count the number of objects in each box. Then color the same number.

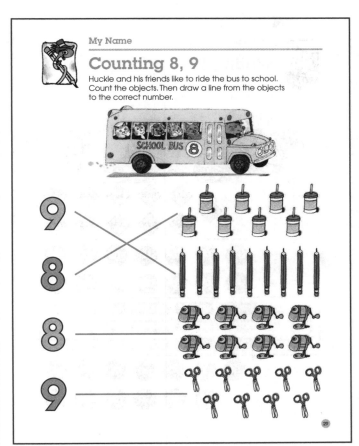

My Name _____

Counting 8, 9

Huckle and his friends like to ride the bus to school. Count the objects. Then draw a line from the objects to the correct number.

My Name _____

Writing 8, 9

Huckle pumps air into his tire. Stop, Huckle, stop! Your tire will pop! Trace the numbers below. Then write them on the lines.

My Name _____

Counting to 10

Lowly helps Huckle put out safety cones. Careful, Lowly! Count the number of cones in each box. Then color the same number.

Writing 10

Bridget thinks Goldbug is going too fast. Watch out, Goldbug! Trace the number 10. Then write 10 on the lines provided. Next, cross out the objects in each group so there are ten things left.

What Comes Before?

Help Huckle and Lowly find the correct speed limits. In the blank space in each box, write the number that comes before the number shown. The first one has been done for you.

What Comes After?

More speed limit signs are missing! Help Goldbug find them. In the blank space in each box, write the number that comes after the number shown. The first one has been done for you.

Counting 1-10

Huckle, Lowly, and Bridget like to count forward and backward! Help them fill in the missing numbers.

Counting Backward

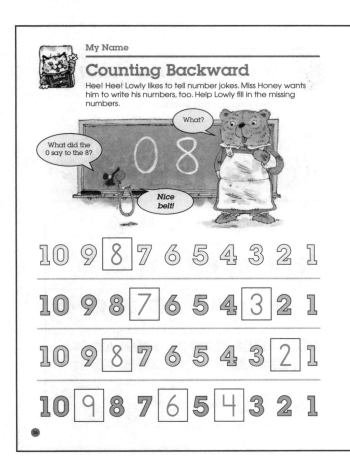

My Name

Hee! Hee! Lowly likes to tell number jokes. Miss Honey wants him to write his numbers, too. Help Lowly fill in the missing numbers.

What did the 0 say to the 8?

What?

Nice belt!

10 9 8 7 6 5 4 3 2 1

10 9 8 7 6 5 4 3 2 1

10 9 8 7 6 5 4 3 2 1

10 9 8 7 6 5 4 3 2 1

Which Number Is Greater?

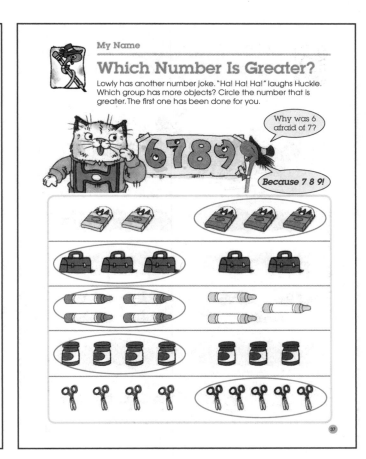

My Name

Lowly has another number joke. "Ha! Ha! Ha!" laughs Huckle. Which group has more objects? Circle the number that is greater. The first one has been done for you.

Why was 6 afraid of 7?

Because 7 8 9!

| flags | ① 2 3 | cars | ⑦ 8 9 |
| cones | ④ 5 6 | racers | ⑧ 9 10 |

Which Group Has Fewer?

My Name

Oh, no! Arthur's stuff is falling out of his car! Now he has less in his car than out of it. In each row below, circle the group that has fewer objects. The first one has been done for you.

Which Group Has Fewer?

It's not safe to read and drive, Molly! Look out! Circle the group that has fewer objects. The first one has been done for you.

Which Group Has More?

Oh, no! Frances's car is losing a little candy. Now it's losing a lot of candy! In each of the rows below, circle the group that has more candy. The first one has been done for you.

What Comes Next?

Look out! Lowly is making patterns with shapes and he just broke the chalk! In the row below, color the shape that comes next in the pattern. The first one has been done for you.

What Comes Next?

Ella is behind Bridget, and Molly is behind Ella. Who is next? Goldbug! Color the car that comes next in the patterns below. The first one has been done for you.

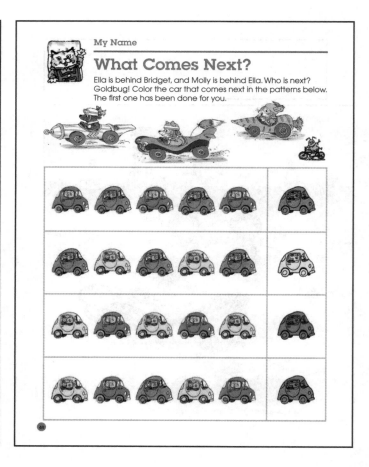

62

Above, Below, and Next to

Today is race day—hooray! Circle the objects that are above Huckle. Put an X on the objects that are next to Huckle. Put a check mark on the objects that are below Huckle. Use the checklist to help you.

Object Checklist:	chair	clock	airplane
	poster	box	bed
	ball	backpack	train

45

Above, Below, and Next to

Yippee! Huckle and Lowly win the race! Circle the objects that are above Lowly. Put an X on the objects that are next to Lowly. Put a check mark on the objects that are below Lowly. Use the checklist to help you.

Object Checklist:	pole	flower	safety cone
	banner	bird	Goldbug's flag
	leaf	butterfly	post

46

Graphing

Help! The race is about to start! Does Goldbug have everything ready? Count the objects in each group. Then color the same number of squares in that row. The first one has been done for you.

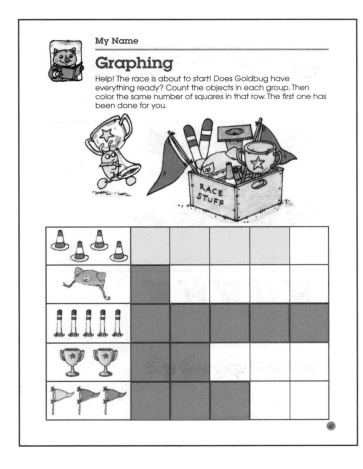

47

Graphing

Time to race! First, Huckle makes sure he has all of his tools. Count the objects in each group. Then color the same number of squares in that column. The first one is done for you.

48

My Name _____

Addition with Sums Up to 4

Count how many objects are in the first group. Write the number under the picture. Count the objects in the second group. Write the number under the picture. Now count the objects in both groups together. Write the number in the box. The first one has been done for you.

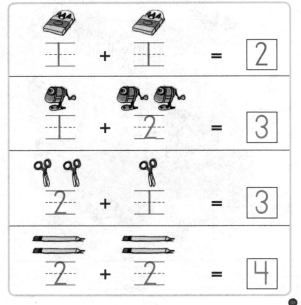

1 + 1 = 2

1 + 2 = 3

2 + 1 = 3

2 + 2 = 4

My Name _____

Addition with Sums Up to 5

Count how many objects are in the first group. Write the number under the picture. Count the objects in the second group. Write the number under the picture. Now count the objects in both groups together. Write the number in the box. The first one has been done for you.

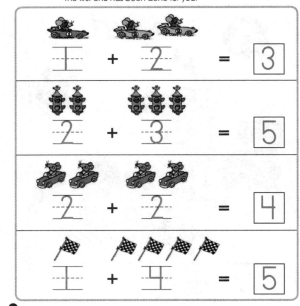

1 + 2 = 3

2 + 3 = 5

2 + 2 = 4

1 + 4 = 5

My Name _____

Subtraction Through 4

Molly likes to play jacks! She picks some up and some are left. Count the total number of objects. Then count the number of objects that are not crossed out. That is the number of objects left. Write the number in the box. The first one has been done for you.

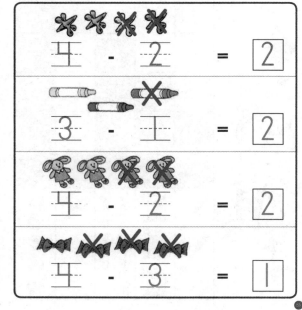

4 - 2 = 2

3 - 1 = 2

4 - 2 = 2

4 - 3 = 1

My Name _____

Subtraction Through 5

Bye-bye! The cars are driving away! Count the number of cars that are not crossed out. That is the number of cars that are left. Write the number in the box. The first one has been done for you.

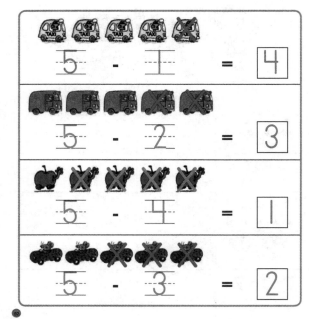

5 - 1 = 4

5 - 2 = 3

5 - 4 = 1

5 - 3 = 2

© Richard Scarry Corporation

STOP

SLOW

YIELD

© Richard Scarry Corporation

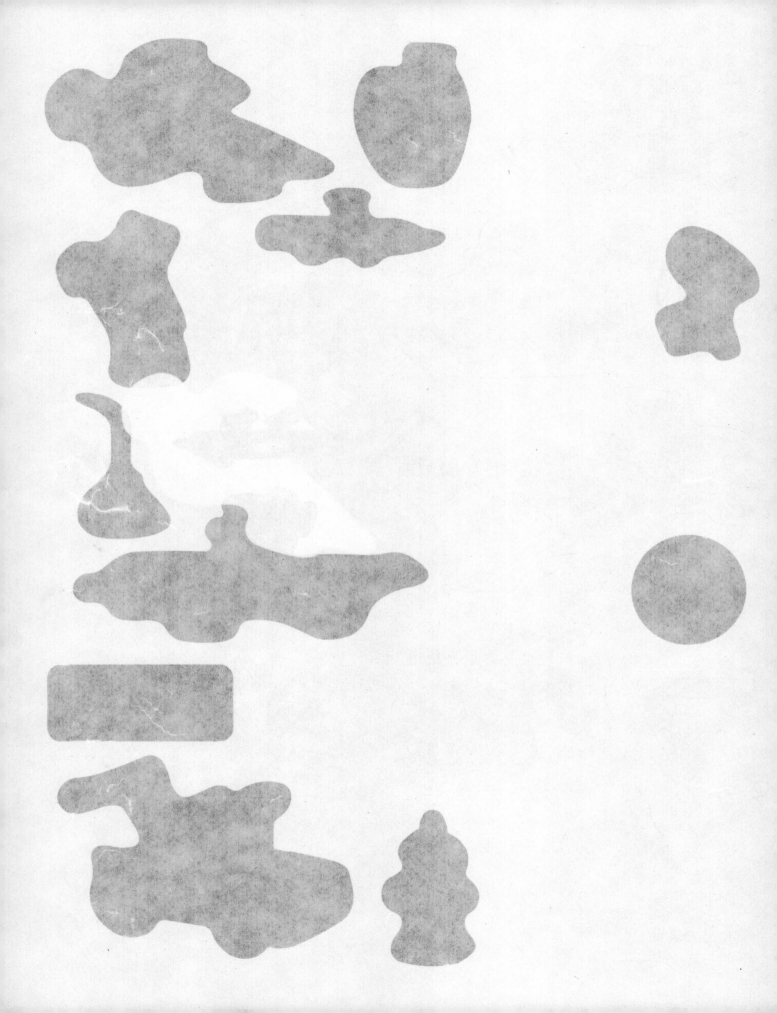